The Little Flower

by Linda Tracey Brandon
illustrated by Lynne Woodcock Cravath

To my siblings,
Jim, Doug, and Elaine, and their spouses,
Malissa, Robin, and Milo—L.T.B.

For Jessica, Sienna, and Kiva, with love
—L.W.C.

A Random House PICTUREBACK®

Random House 🏠 New York

Text copyright © 1997 by Linda Tracey Brandon. Illustrations copyright © 1997 by Lynne Woodcock Cravath.
All rights reserved under International and Pan-American Copyright Conventions.
Published in the United States by Random House, Inc., New York, and simultaneously in Canada
by Random House of Canada Limited, Toronto.
http://www.randomhouse.com/

Library of Congress Cataloging-in-Publication Data
Brandon, Linda Tracey.
The little flower girl / by Linda Tracey Brandon ; illustrated by Lynne Woodcock Cravath.
p.   cm. — (A Random House pictureback)
SUMMARY: Louisa is excited to be the flower girl at Uncle Jim's wedding.
ISBN 0-679-87695-2 [1. Weddings—Fiction.] I. Cravath, Lynne Woodcock, ill. II. Title.
PZ7.B7369Li 1997   [E]—dc20   96-2559
Printed in the United States of America   10 9 8 7 6 5 4 3 2 1

Uncle Jim was finally getting married.

"Louisa, would you be the flower girl in my wedding?" he asked.

Louisa was so excited that she jumped up and down.

"Yes, yes, yes!" she shouted. Louisa had never been to a wedding before.

She stopped jumping. "What does a flower girl do?" she asked.

"We'll tell you later," said Uncle Jim. "Don't worry about it right now."

First Louisa's mother measured Louisa for her flower-girl dress.

"Am I the right size for the dress?" wondered Louisa.

"I will be making your dress," said Mother. "It will be a perfect fit for you."

Then Mother went to measure Louisa's brother, George, for his little black suit. George was two and a half years old. Uncle Jim had asked him to be the ring bearer in his wedding.

George tried to hide from his mother.

"Let's try it on," said Mother when she had finished the dress.
Louisa stepped into it and her mother zipped the zipper.

Louisa glanced in the mirror. She saw a girl who looked a lot like
a fairy princess.

"Can I wear it now?" she asked her mother excitedly.

Mother shook her head.

"Not until the wedding," she said.

Louisa thought the wedding would never happen. Her brother, George, never thought about the wedding at all.

One day Mother said, "The wedding is this weekend."

Suddenly Louisa felt shy. "But I don't know *how* to be a flower girl!" she cried. "What if I trip when I'm walking down the aisle? What if I forget to throw the flower petals? What if everybody laughs?"

"No one will laugh," said Mother. "And you'll learn just what to do at the wedding rehearsal."

The next day Father drove Louisa and George to the church.

"A rehearsal is like a wedding, except that there are no guests and the people don't dress up in their wedding clothes," Father explained. "A rehearsal shows you where you will have to walk and stand."

The church looked very grand to Louisa.

"It's so big!" she said to George. "I bet lots of people are going to be at this wedding. And all those people will watch *us* walk down the aisle."

George pulled his shirt up over his head. Louisa sighed. She knew how George felt.

Inside the church stood the bridesmaids and ushers.

Uncle Jim the groom was there, and so was Melissa the bride.

A nice man explained to Louisa what she would be doing. "You will follow behind the bridesmaids and in front of the bride," he said. "Walk slowly down the aisle in time with the music. You will carry a basket of rose petals and scatter a few of them at a time. It's easy to do," he added, smiling.

"What if I run out of petals before the end?" Louisa asked.

"You won't run out," the nice man said. "But even if you do, it won't matter. Nobody will notice."

"But *I'll* notice," Louisa thought.

George had trouble behaving himself. He didn't want to
carry the little white pillow with the rings on it.
He threw himself on the floor and stared at the ceiling.
The nice man didn't see George and stepped on him.

The next day was the wedding.

Mother had braided and curled Louisa's hair
and then pinned flowers in it.

Louisa felt as if she were floating in her
flower-girl dress and her brand-new shoes.

"Can I wear lipstick?" she asked.

"Just a little," said Mother.

Mother squeezed George
into his little black suit.

There were lots of excited people at the church when Louisa
and her family arrived.

The bridesmaids wore long yellow gowns and carried flowers.
The ushers wore black suits.

Louisa felt very small and scared among all the yellow gowns
and black suits.

"I can't do it!" she thought. "I'll never remember to do everything right."
Her face felt hot and her stomach was twisted into knots. She decided that
she didn't like weddings very much at all.

A long white gown floated in front of Louisa. Inside the gown was
Melissa the bride.

"I know you're nervous, Louisa," whispered Melissa. "I'm nervous, too."

Louisa laughed.

Melissa smiled. "After the wedding, we will be part of the same family.
I will be your new aunt. Is that okay with you, Louisa?"

"Yes!" whispered Louisa.

Music was playing inside the church.

The bridesmaids and ushers walked slowly down the aisle. Everyone turned to watch them.

Louisa was next. Her heart beat faster and faster. Everybody was looking at her!

Then she saw her parents wave. Louisa felt a little better. "Step slowly, step slowly, drop petals!" she repeated to herself. "Step slowly, step slowly, drop petals! Not too many at a time!"

Halfway down the aisle, Louisa noticed that everyone was smiling at her. "Even people that I don't know!" she thought. She smiled and held her chin a little higher.

And she didn't run out of rose petals after all.

George walked down the aisle with the pillow over his face.
Luckily, the rings were tied down.